SHERLOCK'S NIGHT BEFORE CHRISTMAS

A MYSTERY

JULIE PETERSEN

ILLUSTRATED BY

SHERYL DICKERT

GIBBS SMITH

TO ENRICH AND INSPIRE HUMANKIND

'Twas the night before Christmas
on old Baker Street
And Watson and Sherlock were
quick on their feet,
For a Moriarty fiend
was organizing thefts
And leaving his poor victims
stunned and bereft.

Sherlock and Watson were
stalking their man,
Whose deeds seemed a clue
to a much darker plan,
When Sherlock's keen eyes
then observed up ahead
An unfortunate woman
there pleading for bread.

Hustling and harried,
  the shoppers passed by,
But then one kindly soul
  gave compassion a try.
As she reached in her purse
  and pulled out a small offering,
John Watson saw something
  that left him exclaiming,

"Why, Sherlock, I just saw
Santa standing right there!"
But as Sherlock looked over,
the sidewalk was bare.
No jolly old elf did our
Sherlock now see.
Had Watson really seen him
on this Christmas Eve?

Sherlock shook his head
as the pair scurried on.
"You oft get excited,
my good friend Watson.
You're merely caught up
in the lore of the season;
The bustle can make many
lose all their reason."

Cheerful singing was heard
as they went down the street,
"Glorias" and "fa-la-las,"
a children's choir sweet.
When there, quite merrily,
up at their head
Santa led the choir in his
suit of bright red.

At the sight our dear Watson
again cried in surprise,
"Look! There is Santa,
right before our very eyes!"
Quickly, Sherlock turned his head,
but nothing did he see.
He thought, *John isn't prone to fibbing,
so how could this be?*

Not a trace of St. Nick
did their searching reveal.
"Perhaps," put forth John,
"this Santa is for real!"
"Nonsense," said Sherlock.
"'Tis a man in disguise.
I can't believe he's real
until I see with my eyes.

"You recall, my dear Watson,
that time when we found
The Baskerville mystery
was no ghostly hound
But in fact, a poor dog
all costumed and arrayed.
This Santa Claus fantasy is,
as well, a charade."

Suddenly, the thief out from
an alley did dash!
Posthaste our detectives
picked up the chase in a flash.
Heedless, they pursued him
through the holiday crowd,
But the thief into a clutch
of fine gentlemen plowed.

Their top hats and canes tumbled
all across the road,
And the thief's clumsy progress
was effectively slowed
Just enough for smart Sherlock
to grab him from behind
And hold onto his collar while
Watson bound his wrists tight.

A crowed gathered 'round
  until the bobbies came
And interrogated the thief
  about his miscreant endgame.
The thief then a warning
  to Sherlock did impart
From his boss, Moriarty,
  who had schemed from the start:

"Just when you think you have
given your all,
Moriarty will meet you,
eventually, at the fall."
With this, the thief said
not a single word more.
The bobbies took him away.
Calm descended, as before.

People maneuvered on their own journeys and ways.
There was still much to do before tomorrow, Christmas Day!

On the street, a small group for donations did behest.
Watson opened his wallet to give per their request.

"Why," scoffed Sherlock, "do you
give in to such sentiment?"
At the query, Watson paused,
his answer was . . . hesitant.
"As I have received kindnesses,
I pass on charity.
'Tis a blessing to impart
of my ample prosperity."

"Did you not see Santa
there with them standing?"
"No!" replied Sherlock,
his eyes the scene scanning.
And still, he could not see
any evidence of Claus.
His thoughts were now whirling
and swirling without pause.

No footprints, nor pipe smoke,
nor sound of the merry man.
Yet thrice had John seen him
in just a short time span!
Why can John Watson see him,
and I, Sherlock, not?
No theory gave Sherlock
the answers he sought.

On their way back home,
the wind turned rain to sleet.
The sidewalks grew slick
as they walked along the street.
Out of a shop, a woman
gingerly stepped.
But as she strode to the sidewalk,
her feet lost their grip!

Down to the ground
the shopper fell with a thud.
Her coat was all covered
with brown guck and mud.
Posthaste, Sherlock lifted her
up to her feet,
As Watson collected her
gifts from the street.

She thanked them for helping her,
ever so sweetly.
As she did, Sherlock glimpsed
a bright flash of red, fleetly.
Not more did he see,
though his eyes opened wide.
But Watson again said
he'd there Santa spied.

CLAUS?

Sherlock was amazed, stunned,
and just a bit vexed.
Whatever Watson was seeing
sure had him perplexed!
It wasn't impossible—
for Sherlock caught a glimpse too—
It seems so improbable,
but maybe Santa is true!

"My good fellow, Watson,
will you please pardon me?
I didn't believe you;
but I *think* I did see.
I'm not sure just how,
nor understand the reason,
But there's something quite special
about this holiday season."

Doctor Watson smiled;
his forgiveness wasn't needed.
His affection for Sherlock
remained unimpeded.

They split up for a while,
then back home on Baker Street,
That night Sherlock wrapped gifts
by the fireplace heat.

For his friend Doctor Watson
he got a new book.
A tea set for Mrs. Hudson,
his housekeeper and cook—
Thoughtful gifts for those people
who he esteemed most,
Who'd lent him support when
by mysteries he was engrossed.

At the rustling of the tree
swiftly Sherlock turned 'round—
But no dastardly criminal
was there to be found—
Instead, there stood Santa Claus,
dressed in red with white fur.
Sherlock blinked and pinched
himself—just to be sure.

Yes, it was the jolly man,
brushing off and smiling.
"Indeed, sir" said Santa,
"Watson has me been spying.
I'm ever present, noting each
good, kindly deed,
Be it for friend, or family,
or neighbor in need."

"The true meaning of Christmas
is compassion and love,
When selfishness and ego
are freely let go of.
Each deed is a gift greater than
what's under a tree,
Those who give these great gifts
are then able to see me."

For Sherlock, at last,
the mystery had become clear
Of what made the season
so special each year.
Then Santa flew into
the dwindling light.
"Merry Christmas, Sherlock Holmes,
and to all a good night."

First Edition
22 21 20 19 18 5 4 3 2 1

Published by
Gibbs Smith
P.O. Box 667
Layton, Utah 84041

1.800.835.4993 orders
www.gibbs-smith.com

Designed and illustrated by Sheryl Dickert
Printed and bound in China

Gibbs Smith books are printed on either recycled, 100% post-consumer waste, FSC-certified papers or on paper produced from sustainable PEFC-certified forest/controlled wood source. Learn more at www.pefc.org.

Library of Congress Control Number:
2018930889
ISBN 978-1-4236-4980-9